24 Hour Telephone Renewals 0845 071 4343
HARINGEY LIBRARIES

THIS BOOK MUST BE RETURNED ON OR BEFORE
THE LAST DATE MARKED BELOW

CJ

To

7 OCT 2008

12 OCT 2009

12 OCT 2009

- 7 DEC 2009

1 3 JUL 2010

2 5 AUG 2010

0 3 SEP 2010

OCT 2010

1 5 NOV 2010

0 7 DEC 2010

0 4 NOV 2011

0 9 JAN 2012

1 4 AUG 2012

0 4 SEP 2012

- 9 JUL 2014

2 1 AUG 2017

1 9 NOV 2019

1 5 APR 2013

0 9 SEP 2013

RES 4 29/10

1 8 NOV 2014

2 0 AUG 2015

2 2 DEC 2016

0 4 MAR 2017

0 4 MAR 2017

1 8 MAR 2017

2 1 JUN 2017

- 7 DEC 2017

ine renewals at libraries haringey gov.uk

D1422765

245135 9

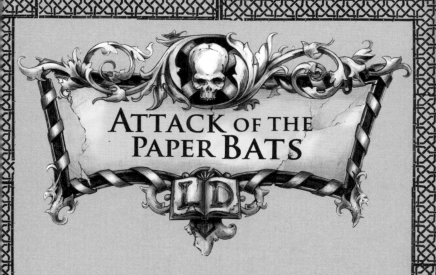

ATTACK OF THE PAPER BATS

BY MICHAEL DAHL
ILLUSTRATED BY MARTÍN BLANCO

Librarian Reviewer
Laurie K. Holland
Media Specialist

Reading Consultant
Elizabeth Stedem
Educator/Consultant

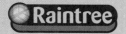

Raintree is an imprint of Capstone Global Library Limited, a
company incorporated in England and Wales having its registered
office at 7 Pilgrim Street, London, EC4V 6LB – Registered
company number: 6695582

"Raintree" is a registered trademark of Pearson Education
Limited, under licence to Capstone Global Library Limited

Text © Stone Arch Books, 2009
First published by Stone Arch Books in 2007
First published in hardback in the United Kingdom in 2009
The moral rights of the proprietor have been asserted.

Art Director: Heather Kinseth
Cover Graphic Designer: Brann Garvey
Interior Graphic Designer: Kay Fraser
Edited in the UK by Laura Knowles
Printed and bound in China by Leo Paper Products Ltd

ISBN 978-1406212662 (hardback)

13 12 11 10 09
10 9 8 7 6 5 4 3 2 1

British Library Cataloguing in Publication Data
Dahl, Michael.
Attack of the paper bats. -- (Library of doom)
813.5'4-dc22
A full catalogue record for this book is available
from the British Library.

TABLE OF CONTENTS

he Library of Doom is the world's largest collection of strange and dangerous books. The Librarian's duty is to keep the books from falling into the hands of those who would use them for evil purposes.

CHAPTER 1

A book lies open on the street.

The book belongs to the Library of Doom. It was stolen from the Library many years ago.

It travelled through many lands, passing from person to person.

The breath of a thousand readers mixed with the ink and sighed through the paper.

———◆———

After many years, a young boy saw the book in the window of a small shop.

"That's the book I want," said the boy.

As the boy hurried home with his new purchase, the book fell out of his bag.

Now, the book lies in the street.
Its pages grow **warm** in the pale
moonlight.

8

CHAPTER 2

A STRANGE WIND

From out of nowhere, a cold
wind blows down the street.

The wind shuffles the pages of the book. Several pages rip off.

The wind's invisible fingers fold and refold the pages into strange and deadly shapes.

The pages are sharp. The pages fly by themselves.

The pages are **hungry**.

On the **dark** street, the wind rips off more pages.

❰ CHAPTER 3 ❱

DARK WINDOWS

In another part of the dark city, the Librarian walks alone.

The wind **whistles** down the street.

The Librarian pulls up his collar. He lowers his head as he walks into the wind.

As the Librarian stops in front of bookshops, he peers into the dark windows.

"None of these have the books I want," he whispers to himself.

The Librarian is searching
for books that were lost or stolen
from the Library of Doom.

A piece of paper flies overhead
in the wind.

A **scream** rips through
the dark.

17

CHAPTER 4

THE SCREAM

In another street, a young boy is reading a book.

He hears something scratch softly against his window.

The boy opens his window.

A small dark shape falls out of the sky.

"Ow!" yells the boy. A sharp piece of paper slashes his hand.

The boy tries to close the window, but the wind is too strong. More and more pieces of paper rush into his room.

They move as if they were not pieces of paper, but bats.

The boy **screams**.

(CHAPTER 5)

ATTACK!

The Librarian runs down a
lonely alley.

He runs towards the sound of
the scream.

Looking up, the Librarian sees
a cloud of pages.

Some of them are **flying** into
a small window high above him.

Somehow he must help the boy.

The Librarian leaps and grabs
the bottom of a fire escape. Quickly,
he darts up the metal ladder.

The Librarian crouches and then leaps. He flies across the alley.

As he leaps into the swarming ball of paper, the creatures attack.

He is surrounded.

The Librarian leans backwards.
He loses his balance and **falls**
into the alley.

❨ CHAPTER 6 ❩

THE RIVER

The boy leans out of his window.

He watches the paper bats leave his room and attack the man who tried to help him.

On the floor of the alley, the Librarian covers his head and face with his long, dark coat. Then he runs.

He cannot see where he is going, but he knows he cannot fight the swarm of pages.

The Librarian rushes down the alley. The alley drops off into a **dark** river.

The Librarian stops at the end
of the alley, and then **dives**.

The pages dive after him.

In the water, the pages lose their sharp edges. The paper **falls apart**.

Everything sinks to the bottom
of the river.

In his room, the young boy looks
through the closed window.

Where is the **strange** man
who tried to rescue him?

THE END

33

A PAGE FROM THE LIBRARY OF DOOM

PAPER

The word "paper" comes from "papyrus," a plant that grew along the River Nile in Egypt. Ancient Egyptians peeled strips from the tall plants and pounded them flat to write on.

Ts'ai Lun, a member of the Chinese emperor's court in 105 CE, is honored as the inventor of paper. He chopped up bamboo, bark from mulberry trees, and even fishing nets, to make a pulpy substance. When the pulp dried, it looked like our modern paper.

Today, paper is made from fibres that come mostly from trees, but can also come from straw or cotton.

Every year, the average person in the UK uses more than 200 kilograms of paper!

Paper is dangerous! Brothers Homer and Langley Collyer never threw anything away. One day in 1947, they were found dead in their New York apartment buried under fallen stacks of old newspapers. It took rescuers 18 days to recover the bodies from beneath all the paper.

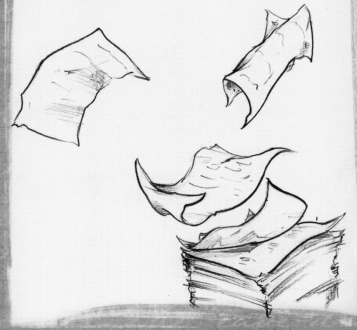

ABOUT THE AUTHOR

Michael Dahl is the author of more than 100 books for children and young adults. He has twice won the AEP Distinguished Achievement Award for his non-fiction. His Finnegan Zwake mystery series was chosen by the Agatha Awards to be among the five best mystery books for children in 2002 and 2003. He collects books on poison and graveyards, and lives in a haunted house in Minneapolis, USA.

ABOUT THE ILLUSTRATOR

Martín Blanco was born in Argentina and studied drawing and painting at the Fine Arts University of Buenos Aires. He is currently a freelance illustrator and lives in Barcelona, Spain where he is working on films and comic books. Blanco loves to read, especially thrillers and horror. He also enjoys playing football, the Barcelona football team, and playing the drums with his friends.

GLOSSARY

dart (DART) – to move quickly

peer (PEER) – to stare, or look carefully

shuffle (SHUF-uhl) – to move something quickly from one place to another. A person might shuffle through the pages of a phone book, searching for a certain telephone number.

swarm (SWORM) – to move together in a big group. Flies swarm; so do bees.

DISCUSSION QUESTIONS

1. At the beginning of the story, a young boy buys the strange book that ends up in the street. Do you think the book landed in the street on purpose? Do you think the book knew what it was doing? Explain.

2. Why do you think the paper bats stopped attacking the boy and went after the Librarian instead?

3. What do you think happened to the Librarian after he dived into the river? What happened to the boy who was attacked?

WRITING PROMPTS

1. The paper bats all came from the same book, but we never learn what that book is about. What do you think? Use your own ideas and describe the kind of book it is. What is the book's title? What is it about? Does it have pictures? Would you want to read it?

2. What would the Librarian have done if there was no river nearby? How else could he have destroyed the swarm of paper bats? Write down another way he might have defeated them.

MORE BOOKS TO READ

This story may be over, but there are many more dangerous adventures in store for the Librarian. Will the Librarian be able to escape the cave of the deadly giant bookworms? Will he defeat the rampaging Word Eater in time to save the world? You can only find out by reading the other books from the Library of Doom...

The Beast Beneath the Stairs
The Book that Dripped Blood
Cave of the Bookworms
The Creeping Bookends
Escape from the Pop-up Prison
The Eye in the Graveyard
The Golden Book of Death
Poison Pages
The Smashing Scroll
The Twister Trap
The Word Eater